SPOTLIGHT ON
AN EQUITABLE WORLD

RESPONSIBILITY AND YOUR WORLD

Mary Ratzer

ROSEN PUBLISHING

Published in 2025 by The Rosen Publishing Group, Inc.
2544 Clinton Street, Buffalo, NY 14224

First Edition

Editor: Greg Roza
Book Design: Michael Flynn

Photo Credits: Cover Halfpoint/Shutterstock.com; cover, p. 3 (hands) Dedraw Studio/Shutterstock.com; (series Earth icon) v4ndhira/Shutterstock.com; p. 5 Rawpixel.com/Shutterstock.com; p. 6 Inu/Shutterstock.com; p. 7 Iryna Inshyna/Shutterstock.com; p. 9 mangostock/Shutterstock.com; pp. 10, 17 Monkey Business Images/Shutterstock.com; p. 11 pikselstock/Shutterstock.com; p. 13 Africa Studio/Shutterstock.com; p. 14 Marian Weyo/Shutterstock.com; p. 15 PeopleImages.com - Yuri A/Shutterstock.com; p. 18 Kristi Blokhin/Shutterstock.com; p. 19 Kerry Lane/Shutterstock.com; p. 21 Glynnis Jones/Shutterstock.com; p. 22 bleakstar/Shutterstock.com; p. 23 Dragon Images/Shutterstock.com; p. 25 David Cardinez/Shutterstock.com; p. 26 https://commons.wikimedia.org/wiki/File:%22Mother%22_Jones_and_her_army_of_striking_textile_workers_starting_out_for_their_descent_on_New_York_The_textile_workers_of_Philadelphia_say_they_intend_to_show_the_people_of_the_country_their_LCCN2015649893.jpg; p. 27 Brent Olson/Shutterstock.com; p. 29 Indypendenz/Shutterstock.com.

Cataloging-in-Publication Data

Names: Ratzer, Mary Boyd.
Title: Responsibility and your world / Mary Ratzer.
Description: Buffalo, NY : Rosen Young Adult, 2025. | Series: Spotlight on an equitable world | Includes glossary and index.
Identifiers: ISBN 9781499477344 (pbk.) | ISBN 9781499477184 (library bound) | ISBN 9781499477023 (ebook)
Subjects: LCSH: Social change--Juvenile literature. | Youth--Political activity--Juvenile literature. | Youth movements--Juvenile literature.
Classification: LCC HM831.R38 2025 | DDC 303.4--dc23

Manufactured in the United States of America

Some of the images in this book illustrate individuals who are models. The depictions do not imply actual situations or events.

CPSIA Compliance Information: Batch #CSRYA25. For further information contact Rosen Publishing at 1-800-237-9932.

CONTENTS

Chapter One

IDEAS TO ACTIONS

Responsibility develops as you grow and mature. You are responsible for your schoolwork and your health. You are responsible for your choices and decisions. Many young people feel responsible for the environment. Their values, actions, and choices make a difference. Many students your age are aware of the needs of others in their community. Their actions and choices can support those in need.

Students just like you have strong opinions about issues in their community or world. Your experiences in life will give you ideas for how to change problems you see in the world. Engaging as active citizens, students identify what is meaningful to them. They use skills and partnerships to research and understand problems. They set goals. Engaging with others or alone, they plan solutions and make change happen. Reflecting, they learn from successes and challenges. Their ideas become action.

As an inspiring example, students in east Los Angeles worked for equity in schools serving Hispanic students. They joined together to get leaders to pay attention to inequity. Sixteen students in Montana went to court and won a lawsuit to protect the environment. The students from Marjory Stoneman Douglas High School in Parkland, Florida, started a youth-led movement to stop gun violence after they experienced an active shooter in their school.

What issues do you care about? Why do you care about them? What changes do you want to see in your school, community, nation, or world? What can or should be done? Can you see yourself as a change maker?

Can you identify the things about your community that you think need to change? Perhaps there's a stray dog problem, or a lack of community resources for people experiencing depression. What do you feel strongly about?

Chapter Two

LEARNING SOCIAL RESPONSIBILITY

Learning social responsibility means understanding the ways you're connected to others. It means understanding the ways you depend on others and the ways they depend on you. As an adolescent, you become aware of social responsibility by seeing it in the real world. Deciding who you are and where you fit in your world leads to social responsibility. Engaging in your community to practice social responsibility is like riding a bike with training wheels. The moment you ride without those extra wheels is the moment you have confidence in what you can do. It works the same way with responsibility.

Being a responsible person can seem like a hard thing to achieve. That's why, just like riding a bike, you need to practice.

When you were younger, you could say: "I'm just a kid." Now you're growing up with experiences that teach you how to be responsible. Role models in your family and community influence your sense of responsibility. Volunteering to take on responsible roles and obligations gives you a chance to learn from experience. A life lesson in reaching personal responsibility is that challenges and stress are useful and important. You get stronger by taking on difficult tasks outside your comfort zone. You even learn from failure.

Adolescents take a sharp turn in their path to adulthood when they move from a self-centered view of life to one that includes empathy and concern for others. A focus on others and their needs motivates you, and you begin to see yourself as the one who is responsible. You see yourself as able to do what is needed to ensure the rights of others.

Chapter Three

SERVICE LEARNING

The first step in being a change maker is caring. This is the moment you decide to be a part of a solution and not remain indifferent. When young people volunteer and contribute to their community, good things happen. When young people collaborate to reach out, the benefits multiply. If you have been a part of sharing your time and abilities, you know the rewards. Becoming an active citizen often requires learning how to serve your community.

You can build your skills and confidence if your school offers service learning as a part of a course or club. Many students across the nation benefit from the opportunity to connect with their community through service learning. By connecting with others with a sense of purpose, you develop new skills, perspectives, and confidence. You learn how to collaborate, investigate problems, and bring skills from the classroom to the real world. You can make choices and shape your own goals.

Service learning promotes equity by bringing together students from different backgrounds and strengths. A common purpose unifies and motivates diverse groups. The community itself is the learning environment. Teachers, community members, and students make positive things happen beyond the walls of the school.

The benefits extend from the learners to the community. Many students can be a part of reaching out to others in this way. Sharing your energy with others who need support and creating solutions is a giant step in your path from childhood to maturity.

Service learning combines learning with community service. It can help students gain a better understanding and appreciation for diversity and differences in how people live their lives.

Chapter Four

VOICES OF SOME WHO CONTRIBUTE

"I am a member of my school swim team and I volunteer to teach underprivileged kids to swim. I have learned from the children how lucky I am through my life. I have developed relationships with the kids and am excited seeing them learn to love the water." —Mike

"I go up to Harlem in New York City every Tuesday and work with kids in an after-school creative arts program. It's sponsored by a teacher in my school. I share my time and talent with kids who are new to this country just like me. Creativity makes them really happy even if they have many challenges." —Margo

These are just a few of the many positive stories that come from service learning and becoming a responsible person.

"I am pretty good at math and go to Cheryl's Lodge after school a lot to be a homework helper. The lodge is a trailer. It's a place where a lot of kids can go after school. We goof around a lot and have snacks and stuff. But I know math is hard and I make it easy for others." —Noah

"My school has lots of kids who need winter coats. So, two friends and I put a flyer in the mailboxes where I live. We asked for donations of kid-size coats, snow pants, and boots. We picked them up and got some help from our parents washing them. We set up a nice display in front of the cafeteria and the school nurse helped us to let kids pick coats. I think of those coats every time I go outside and know kids aren't freezing." —Jess

Chapter Five

RESPONSIBLE DECISIONS

Responsible decisions make you a part of the solution for achieving equity and justice. Making decisions based on justice and the well-being of yourself and others is the first step in being a responsible person. Look carefully at the list of "I" statements here and decide if you can do the responsible actions that take a stand for what is right. Draw conclusions about what you can do through action. Draw conclusions about goals you can set to be a part of social justice.

- I can see the impact of my choices and goals on my community.
- I reflect on my role to promote personal and community well-being.
- I can have a role as a responsible and caring part of my community.
- I can have problem-solving conversations about injustice.
- I know that biased words and behaviors affect the rights and freedoms of people.
- I can care about how people are treated and have empathy when they are mistreated because of their identities.
- I know how to stand up for myself and for others when faced with unfairness and injustice.
- I can respectfully tell someone when his or her words or actions are biased or hurtful.
- I will speak up or act when I see unfairness, and I will not let others convince me to go along with injustice.
- I will make judgments after analyzing facts and information.
- I will be aware of the consequences of my actions.
- I will work with others to solve personal and social problems and make our world fair.

There are many ways that you and your friends can be responsible members of the community. Volunteering is just one! Can you think of any other?

Chapter Six

KIDS WHO DO GOOD

Jake and Max, twin brothers from New Jersey, founded Kids That Do Good (kidsthatdogood.com). Their passion for equality and responsibility inspired them to search for ways that other kids could make contributions to the needs of others. They were constantly looking for ways to give back and often were disappointed with few opportunities.

Jake and Max have always felt a compassion for others and for giving to charity. They have donated their own birthday gifts to charity. They made donations of computers to the local children's library. They have raised funds to donate to cancer organizations, food pantries, and so much more. When they turned 13, they realized that other kids also wanted to get involved but didn't know how. That's when

Jake and Max's efforts show that anyone can make a difference for the better if they just try!

they came up with the idea of Kids that Do Good. They wanted to be a resource for kids and show that it's quite easy to make a difference in the community. It just takes one person to make a huge impact on someone else's life.

Kids that Do Good has the goal of connecting kids with ways to give back. This web-based tool is a place where kids and their parents can discover ways to participate locally, regionally, or even on a national level. By using this site, kids and families can quickly find opportunities for any age, location, and the type of organization they want to support. There is also guidance for creating your own way to give back. Easy to use and easy to explore, kids can find choices that match their interests and learn about volunteering.

Chapter Seven

SERVICE IDEAS THAT WORK

Having a hard time figuring out how you can become a responsible and caring member of the community? Here are service ideas that you may be interested in.

Volunteer:

- Volunteer to assist as a buddy in a sports program for kids with physical challenges.
- Explore how you could help kids in a local children's hospital.
- Mow an elderly neighbor's lawn for free.
- Volunteer to help at a pet shelter.
- Visit a nursing home and offer to play board games or have a conversation.
- Become a pen pal with a senior in a local assisted-living facility.
- Coach or manage a team of younger players in a sport you know.
- Volunteer at a senior center to be a technology coach.
- Tutor in a neighborhood after-school program.

Donate:

- Get donations of bikes that kids have outgrown and donate them to kids without bikes.
- Donate old clothes and shoes that are still in good shape to a free store in your community.
- Organize a food drive in your school for a food pantry.
- Collect blankets or sleeping bags to donate to homeless shelters for the winter months.

Help the environment:

- Create a team that recycles classroom paper and plastic.
- Adopt a highway and safely pick up trash as a team effort.
- Plant a tree or donate time to community gardens.

Caring counts:

- Create a new student welcome kit. Guide them to the building, cafeteria menu, the clubs and teams, the school calendar, services, and facilities.
- Write cards to deployed soldiers. Organize care packages for military serving overseas.
- Write thank you cards to first responders. Drop by their headquarters with treats.

Attending a new school can be a highly stressful situation. It can be hard just finding your classroom! By welcoming new students and helping them navigate the school, you are being a responsible citizen!

Chapter Eight

POTENTIAL

Reaching your full potential as a person is the path to your best life. Educators, coaches, parents, and friends see who you are now, and who you are becoming. Your identity continues to take shape. Your social skills, self-confidence, and assets launch you toward your potential. That potential is your gift to your community.

After a shooting in her town, Baton Rouge, Louisiana, 6-year-old Rosalyn Baldwin began a mission. She decided to share gratitude and hugs with every law enforcement officer in the country. Traveling to 44 states, she is now 13 and continuing to create new understanding and respect.

Reaching out to people in the community is an important part of police work. As a responsibile citizen, you can return the favor by reaching out to and respecting police officers.

As a young child with deep appreciation for the police officers who protected her, she made up her mind to share that appreciation. Her potential to accomplish this might have seemed small, but her goodwill found a way. Before the shooting, Rosalyn hadn't imagined the potential she had. But a tragic event moved her to take on a seven-year effort for healing and justice. With the support of her family, she is closing in on her goal of reaching officers in all 50 states.

Rosalyn's visits are met with gratitude and warm smiles. Police officers who are strangers line up for their hug. Their potential to serve their communities is recognized. The many challenges of their jobs and the risks they take are recognized. A 13-year-old girl reaching her potential as a person is making that happen.

Chapter Nine

NOT IN MY TOWN!

Studies show that the number of hate crimes is on the rise. Bias based on race, ethnicity, religion, and gender fuels violence and harm. Responsible and active citizens of a community often take a stand against hateful actions. Communities can find ways to stop crimes and support the victims of these acts. Their unified stand shines a bright light on prejudice in their communities.

In Manhattan Beach, California, a burning tire was thrown onto the porch of a Black family. The father got his children to safety and put out the flames. The hateful act resulted in many thousands of dollars of damage. Instead of moving away, the family stayed to work against hate. Why? Their community stepped up and spoke out. Raising money for repairs and publicly standing by the family, the town is working on justice together.

After the fire, 700 community members gathered in the town square to show their support for the family. Hundreds donated money as a reward for information about the case. Manhattan Beach is working to build a safe community for all.

In 2019, school-age students committed 15 percent of all hate crimes, and 22 percent reported being bullied at school. Students across this country have reached the point where they decided to end hateful actions. They stand up and state the goal: "Not in our town!" Finding the support of parents, teachers, and school leaders, they speak up and stand up. They act, seek support from adults, and support the victims. Forming action-based clubs, communicating their goals and expectations, they draw the line on hate.

On March 24, 2018, concerned citizens marched down 6th Avenue in New York City to protest gun violence.

Chapter Ten

RESPONSIBILITY AND SELF-EFFICACY

Self-efficacy is confidence about your ability to do things and take on challenges. Responsibility for yourself and others involves knowing that you can set a goal and work to make it happen. This confidence can apply to becoming an active citizen in your school or community. Self-efficacy is what tells you that you can use your abilities to do things that matter to you.

Being confident about using your strengths and talents is key in deciding to be an ally or an upstander. Having a positive self-image includes having values and beliefs connected with social awareness and civic action. Those values help you make your decisions to act. Once you experience the positive results of your actions or words, your confidence grows.

Once you gain the confidence to make meaningful changes in your community, you can inspire others to follow your efforts.

The next step in your growing sense of self-efficacy is finding a purpose. A public library in Waltham, Massachusetts, has helped teens reach their goals. Although many care deeply and have strong opinions, some teens are unaware of what they can do. Forums called Real Talk were founded by a local teen named Rachel Cosgrove at the library. Teen leaders with strong interests present discussions on social issues. Their audience of peers engages and begins to define a purpose for their own action.

Teens created slogans that finished the phrase "Freedom from" or "Freedom to." This helped teens to focus on social issues they cared about. Focusing on a meaningful issue is the first step in taking on the responsibility to do something and deciding on a goal.

Chapter Eleven

BIG GOALS, SMALL STEPS

You can decide to be responsible for solving a problem. You can see a challenge and decide to make it your challenge. Big goals are achieved through small steps. A powerful example is the teen organization Students Against Destructive Decisions (SADD). SADD is dedicated to the safety and wellness of all students. Using 40 years of expertise to facilitate educational and engaging programming, SADD operates through school and community chapters (such as student clubs) that are dedicated to advocating healthy decision-making.

SADD has proven that young people empowered to help each other can be a positive force in the community. In 1981, a hockey coach at Wayland High School in Massachusetts, Robert Anastas, joined with 15 students responding to the loss of two hockey players in a drunk driving accident. Creating the Contract for Life, the students and coach worked to get kids from ages 12 to 17 to sign a pledge with their parents to never get into a car driven by someone who was under the influence of alcohol or drugs. Parents signed the pledge to always provide safe transportation if their child needs it. By 1982, 12 states had joined the founding team in working to stop destructive decisions. Thousands of students and parents reached out for Contract for Life by 1984.

By 2023, with 8,000 SADD chapters in middle and high schools, 32 million youth live in communities with SADD programs. Projects include peer-led classes and forums, teen workshops, conferences, rallies, prevention education, leadership training, awareness-raising activities, and legislative work.

SADD programs sometimes set up a fake crash site to demonstrate to teens the reality of drinking and driving. It can be a powerful wakeup call.

Chapter Twelve

OLD ENOUGH TO ACT

Youth are leading movements for fairness and justice across the world. They are gathering in large numbers with united voices for environmental concerns, for safety in school, for equity. They are not too young to walk in the footprints of many who came before them.

June 1903, Philadelphia, Pennsylvania

On this date, 100,000 mill workers, including 10,000 children under 15, went on strike. Their goal was to call attention to harsh and dangerous conditions in mills, and to demand a 55-hour work week. To help draw attention to this situation, a labor organizer known as Mother Jones lead nearly 300 child laborers from Philadelphia to the home of President Theodore Roosevelt in Oyster Bay, New York.

Mother Jones stands at the center of child laborers and protestors during their march to President Roosevelt's house in 1903.

Protestors in Salt Lake City, Utah, walk down State Street in solidarity with the Native Americans who engaged in the protest in Standing Rock, North Dakota, in 2016.

May 1963, Birmingham, Alabama

Hundreds of Black Birmingham students marched for civil rights and desegregation of public services. On their way to city hall, police arrested hundreds. The next day more students joined the effort. National media covered the violence that police used to stop the marchers. This march resulted in national support for civil rights.

April 2016, Standing Rock Indian Reservation

A Native American youth group called One Mind Youth Movement blocked construction of the Dakota Access Pipeline. It threatened the main tribal water supply and sacred ancestral lands moving half a million barrels of oil a day under the Missouri River. The protest at Standing Rock, North Dakota, made millions of Americans aware of the injustice.

Chapter Thirteen

DIGITAL TOOLS

The National Education Association confirms that student activism is on the rise. One place where you find evidence of that is online. The energy and empathy of millions of young people shines brightly on the internet. Digital tools propel you into the world of responsible citizens. Their ownership of problems such as mental health, gun safety, education, gender rights, and the environment get powerful results.

Virtually teaming up, their projects produce hundreds of thousands of individual successful actions. Kids engage in action with sites like DoSomething.org, the Youth Activism Project, and Volunteer Match. The Buddy Project uses social media to support teen mental health and prevent suicide. Young people make use of their digital skills and amplify their voices when they join a project launched online. They join others in unified efforts to solve problems affecting youth.

Featuring role models and highlights of their contributions, adolescents see people just like themselves successfully owning and solving problems online. Podcasts and videos share experience and practical guidance for action. Becoming a part of a solution comes with motivated partners already working on projects you might value.

The National Council of Social Studies and many states have worked together to create a graduation certificate, the Seal of Civic Readiness. They have created an online toolkit to provide guidance in using tools for advocacy. The toolkit also features access to resources for real-world active citizenship.

Young activists who belong to diverse communities raise awareness of the changes they are working toward. They can be a powerful source of inspiration for other teens.

Chapter Fourteen

CHECKING IN ON ACTION

Are you uncertain about how responsibility for active citizenship is a fit for someone your age? Are you overwhelmed by the possibilities, risks, and the idea of being ready to solve problems that mean something to you? Review the ways that you might begin to try being an active citizen. Ask yourself if you already are an active citizen. Ask yourself how you might grow in your potential for responsible citizenship in your school or community. Set one goal to accept the challenge of personal social responsibility. Check in on active citizenship using these "I" statements:

- **I take responsibility for standing up to prejudice.**
- **I will act, when it is appropriate and safe, when I see unfairness even if those around me do not.**
- **I will not let others convince me to go along with injustice.**
- **I am concerned about how people are treated.**
- **I will make responsible decisions even when no one else does.**
- **I feel empathy for people who are excluded or mistreated.**
- **I can respectively tell someone when their words or actions are biased or hurtful.**
- **I will communicate with respect even when we disagree.**
- **I will work with family, friends, and community members to make the world fair and just for everyone.**
- **I will be thoughtful and creative in my actions to achieve my goals.**
- **I will plan and coordinate my actions to achieve goals.**
- **I will participate in activities that focus on a classroom, school, community, state, or national problem.**

GLOSSARY

advocacy: The act of supporting a cause.

bias: To have an unfair preference or dislike of something.

collaborate: To work together with others to reach a common goal.

consequence: A result or effect of an action or condition.

depression: A mental disorder marked by sadness, inactivity, and loss of a sense of one's own worth.

empathy: Being aware of and sharing another person's feelings, experiences, and emotions.

equity: Fairness or justice in dealings between persons.

exclude: To leave someone out of an activity or meeting.

gratitude: The state of being grateful.

indifferent: A lack of concern for something.

obligation: Something, such as a promise or contract, that requires one to do something.

perspective: Point of view.

potential: Capable of becoming real.

prejudice: Unfriendly feelings directed against an individual, a group, or a race.

segregation: The separation or isolation of a race, class, or group.

virtual: Occurring or existing online.

volunteer: Offer to do something for free.

INDEX